For Harrison.
Bravely discover life, enjoying the ups and learning from the downs!

Published by Aruna Khanzada

www.arunakhanzada.co.uk
akhanzada.author@gmail.com
www.harrisonbravesthehill.com

Layout by My Red Bag
www.myredbag.uk

Harrison
and
Laila Caterpillar
are

BEST FRIENDS.

They live
at the
bottom of
Primrose Hill.

Harrison and Laila have never been
to the top of Primrose Hill.

Laila knows she has to leave the
bottom of the hill soon.

She has to go to the tree up the hill
to build a cocoon and go to sleep.

Laila worries Harrison will be lonely
when she goes.

One day Laila looks up the hill and
sees a nest in the tree.

There is an egg in the nest.

"Let's go up together and meet
the new family," says Laila.

"Oh no! I couldn't do that. I am not
brave enough to find out what is
up and over the hill!" says Harrison.

So Laila and Harrison stay down at the bottom of the hill where Harrison feels safe.

One night Laila says,

"Harrison, I can't wait any more.
I have to go up to the tree
at the top of the hill
to make a cocoon
and have a long sleep."

Harrison is sad his friend has to go.

"Come with me Harrison!
Let's have an adventure together!"

"Oh no! I couldn't do that. I am not brave enough to find out what is up and over the hill!" says Harrison.

"See you soon Harrison!"
says Laila and
off she goes
to the top of the hill.

She wiggles her way up the
tree at the top of the hill
and she munches on leaves
till she is very full and
very sleepy..... and then....

....she curls up
snug as a bug
into a cosy cocoon
and goes to sleep.

Harrison looks up the hill.
He sees Laila's cocoon
in the tree.

He misses Laila very much.

How he longs to go up
to the top of the hill.

"If only I was brave enough to
climb the hill..."

Along comes Dolly Dog.
Dolly lives in Primrose Hill too.
She loves making new friends.

"Hello little bird.
My name is Dolly.
You do look sad,"
says Dolly.

"Hello, I'm Harrison.
I do feel sad, and lonely too.
I miss my friend Laila who is asleep
in her cocoon in the tree
at the top of the hill."

"Then let's go up to the top of the hill
 and wait for Laila to wake up," says Dolly.

"Oh no! I couldn't do that. I'm not brave enough
to find out what is up and over the hill!"
says Harrison.

So Dolly stays with Harrison
at the bottom of the hill
where Harrison feels safe.

One day the wind blows very hard.
Luckily Laila is safe in her cocoon in the tree.

The wind blows harder and harder.
It blows so hard that the nest in the tree topples.

The egg rolls out and....

DOWN

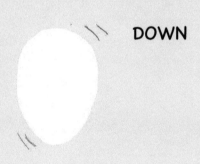

DOWN

DOWN

and it..........

ROLLS.........

and ROLLS..........

and ROLLS...........

All the way down
to the bottom of the hill....

........right by Harrison's feet.

What will Harrison do?

MAYBE.....
......he will do......

NOTHING?

What if it rains?
The egg will get cold!

THAT'S NOT A GOOD IDEA.

Harrison knows
what to do.

He makes a nest.

He puts th   he nest.
Then he
   to ke

One day the egg begins to
CRRR...

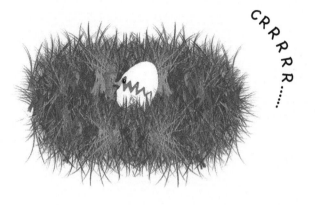

CRRRRR......

......RAAAAA......

......ACCKKK......

mama? papa?

CRACK.........
and out pops a
pretty purple chick!

"Harrison, it is time to be brave," says Dolly.
"We must take the chick up
to the nest at the top of the hill.
Her Mum and Dad must be very worried."

Harrison thinks long and hard.

He is scared. He does not know what is
up and over the hill.

But the chick looks even more scared down
at the bottom of the hill.

She is really missing her Mum and Dad
and she is too little to find them
by herself.

Harrison decides to be brave.

"Yes Dolly, let's go!" he
says.

So....

UP....... they go!

UP.......

UP.......

The higher they go the less scared Harrison feels.

Harrison is getting very excited. He knows Laila will be waking up soon and he can't wait to surprise her!

He has really missed his best friend.

At the top of the hill, Laila has just woken up from her long sleep and she wriggles out of her cosy cocoon.

Laila has become a beautiful butterfly!

She looks down and sees her friend Harrison coming up the hill with Dolly and the chick.

"Harrison! I'm Laila Butterfly now!" she says.

"I'm so happy you braved the hill Harrison. It's AMAZING up at the top!"

"And the view is so NICE.... come see!" says Laila.

Harrison reaches the top of the hill.

He looks down over the other side of the hill and is delighted he decided to be brave.

He finds a WHOLE NEW WORLD................

.......waiting to be discovered.......
with old friends, and new ones too!

I HAVE CONVERSED WITH THE SPIRITU

UN. I

ON PRIMROSE HILL

Lightning Source UK Ltd.
Milton Keynes UK
UKHW020253171118
332470UK00009B/86/P